MW00895720

My Big Day at a michigan state football Game

A memory book of my big day at Spartan Stadium!

Kelley Gottschang and Michele Meissner

Text, Design and Layout © 2010 Mama Tiger, LLC

All rights reserved. No part of this book may be reproduced or transmitted
in any form or by any means, electronic or mechanical, including photocopy,
recording, or any information storage and retrieval systems
without permission in writing from Mama Tiger, LLC,

Printed and bound in U.S.A.

PRT1010A

ISBN-13: 978-1-936319-24-4
ISBN-10: 1-936319-24-1

My Big Day at a Michigan State Football Game is a concept
created and developed by Mama Tiger, LLC.

Published by Mascot Books

Trademarks of the University used under license.

Information deemed reliable, accuracy not guaranteed.

Photo, Illustration and Song Credits
Front Cover Photo, Flags Photo and Sparty Photo © Brian Warkoczeski,
Zeke the Wonder Dog Photo © The Muskegon Chronicle,
Football Illustration © Kelley K. Gottschang,
The MSU Fight Song by Lankey and Sayles,
Zeke the Wonder Dog used by permission of Jim & Terri Foley, www.msualum.com/Zeke/

This book is dedicated to Drew, who constantly inspires and amazes us, to Noah, whose baby shower started it all and to Laurel and Mo, truly, Spartans through and through!

Michele and Kelley

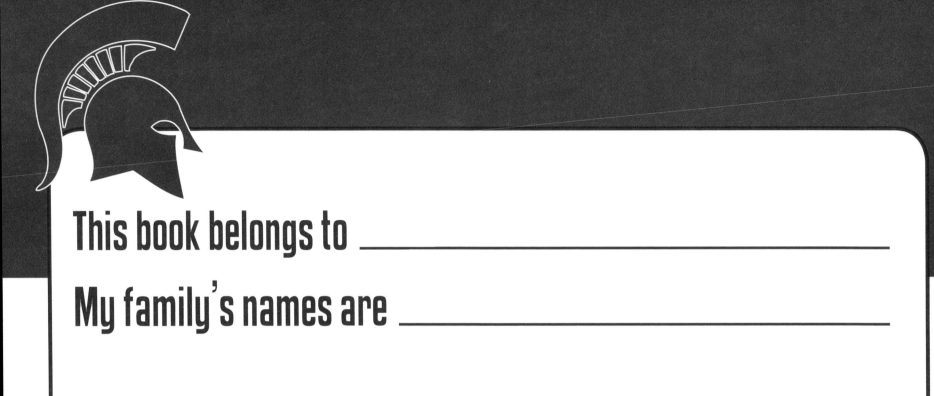

This book belongs to _____

My family's names are _____

_____

_____

_____

Snapshot of me
and my family!

This book was given to me by _____

_____

Snapshot of me and the Michigan State fan(s)
who gave me this awesome book!

I live at _____

_____

**Snapshot of me
where I live!**

The Big Game

My big Michigan State football day was on _____

Michigan State played _____

And beat them by _____

For a final score of _____

Go State!

The Big Game

I went to the game with _____

_____

_____

Snapshot of us at the game!

_____

_____

The Big Game

I was _____ old.

I weighed _____

I was _____ tall.

I wore _____

_____

Snapshot of me in my
Spartan gear!

On My Big Day

I tailgated with _____

_____

We threw the football _____ times.

We ate _____

_____

On My Big Day

I heard the bells chime at Beaumont Tower on game day!

Snapshot of me at Beaumont Tower!

On My Big Day

I crossed the Red Cedar River

on my way to the game!

Snapshot of me crossing
the river!

On My Big Day

I touched The Spartan Statue

on my way to the game!

Snapshot of me with
The Spartan Statue!

On My Big Day

I sat in Section _____ Row _____ Seat _____

Game Attendance _____

I was part of Spartan Nation at the big game today!

On My Big Day

Snapshot of me
in my seat!

Snapshot of the view
from my seat!

On My Big Day

My Michigan State football ticket

Paste my Michigan State football ticket stub here!

On My Big Day

I saw Sparty plant the MSU flag at midfield at the big game!

Snapshot of me looking like Sparty planting the flag!

On My Big Day

The weather was _____

_____

My souvenirs for the day were _____

_____

_____

On My Big Day

I did the Go Green-Go White cheer _____ times.

I sang the Michigan State fight song _____ times.

I did the wave _____ times.

I ate _____

I drank _____

On My Big Day

The coach was _____

The quarterback was _____

The star player was _____

There were _____ total yards of offense!

There were _____ sacks! Go defense!

On My Big Day

At the halftime show,

the MSU band played...

_____

_____

_____

Snapshot of the band during
the halftime show!

When I Grow Up...

and play football for Michigan State, I'm going to play

_____ position on offense!

_____ position on defense!

_____ position on special teams!

When I Grow Up...

I'm going to...

play the _____ in the band!

_____ cheer on the cheerleading team!

_____ be Sparty the Mascot!

The MSU Fight Song

by Lankey and Sayles

On the banks of the Red Cedar,
There's a school that's known to all;
Its specialty is winning,
And those Spartans play good ball;
Spartan teams are never beaten,
All through the game they fight;
Fight for the only colors,
Green and White.

Go right through for MSU,
Watch the points keep growing.
Spartan teams are bound to win,
They're fighting with a vim!
Rah! Rah! Rah!
See their team is weakening,
We're going to win this game,
Fight! Fight! Rah! Team, Fight!
Victory for MSU!

We're both mammals!

Zeke the Wonder Dog

Me!

Snapshot of me smiling
like Zeke!

Snapshots of My Big Day

Snapshots of My Big Day

Autographs

Autographs

Michigan State University Facts

School colors are Green ⬤ and White ⬜ .

School mascot is "Sparty".

Michigan State University and Spartan Stadium are in East Lansing, Michigan.

Spartan Stadium Facts

The MSU football stadium opened in 1923 and had a capacity of 14,000.

In 1935 the stadium was dedicated as Macklin Field after John Macklin, football coach from 1911 to 1915.

Michigan State University joined the Big Ten Conference in 1948 and increased the capacity to 51,000.

In 1957, the stadium's capacity was increased to 76,000 and renamed Spartan Stadium.

On the morning of every home game, the football team walks across campus on the Spartan Walk, a tradition which has the team cross the Red Cedar River, pass the Spartan Statue and enter the stadium.

On October 6, 2001, the stadium hosted 74,554 fans who watched "The Cold War" between Michigan State University and The University of Michigan hockey teams. This record held for almost nine years.

For 54 years, Spartan Stadium has ranked among the NCAA's top 25 in attendance.

On September 3, 2005, an expansion bumped the stadium's capacity to 75,005.

This book is a tribute to the Michigan State fans, players, coaches and staff
that make every Saturday in the fall an amazing adventure.
Sparty On!